# The Lost Legionary

by
**Mick Gowar**

**Illustrations by Martin Remphry**

Watts Books
London • New York • Sydney

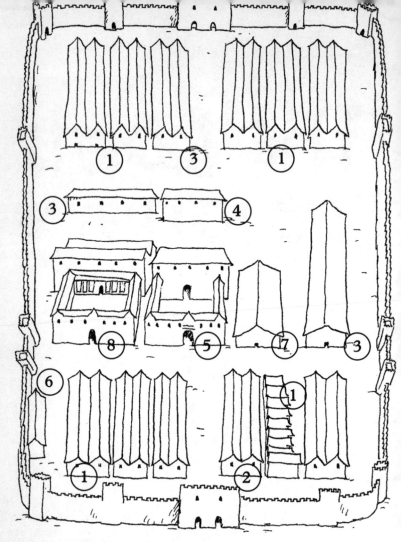

# Map of Housesteads Fort

1 Barracks
2 Bathhouse
3 Workshops
4 Hospital
5 HQ
6 Latrine
7 Granary
8 Commandant's
House

# The Lost Legionary

First published in 1995 by Franklin Watts

Paperback edition published 1997

This edition 1998

Franklin Watts
96 Leonard Street
London EC2A 4RH

Franklin Watts Australia
14 Mars Road
Lane Cove
NSW 2006

Series editor: Paula Borton
Consultant: Joan Blyth
Designer: Kirstie Billingham

A CIP catalogue record for this book
is available from the British Library.

ISBN 0 7496 2629 1 (pbk)
0 7496 2222 9 (hbk)

Dewey Classification 942.01

Printed in Great Britain

# 1

## The Freezing Fort

Gaius stood in the open courtyard at the centre of the big house. He looked up. The sky was sullen and grey. Gaius shivered. Even in the shelter of the courtyard and with his new leather cape on, he was cold. What was keeping his father?

Gaius was excited and impatient. Today he was going to see the fort for the first time. Ever since he could remember, Gaius had dreamed of being a soldier like his father, Marcus - guarding the frontiers of the Empire, fighting barbarians - maybe one day becoming a camp prefect like his

father, or even becoming a legate and commanding a legion of his own!

Suddenly, Gaius was jerked sideways by the long-legged, rough-haired dog at the end of the short leather leash. It dragged him towards the pillared colonnade that ran round the courtyard.

"No, Finn - No!" Gaius tried to sound fierce and determined. But the dog simply ignored Gaius and cocked its leg against one of the pillars.

"I hope nobody's watching," thought Gaius. He waited helplessly for the dog to finish.

Gaius was still trying to pull the dog away when his father strode out into the courtyard.

"Good lad!" said Marcus cheerfully.

Gaius beamed. His father wasn't usually so affectionate.

Marcus bent down and patted the dog
heartily. "Good lad," he repeated.

Marcus straightened up. "Well, my boy," he said to Gaius at last, "now I'm going to show you round your new home." He rubbed his hands together briskly. "It's a bit nippy, but you'll soon get used to it. I'll show you round the fort, then we'll go out and hunt some hare. You'll like that —" he stooped and scratched the big dog behind its ears, "won't you, boy? Come on!"

Marcus led the way back through a doorway and into the bare entrance hall. The dog followed enthusiastically, dragging Gaius behind him.

"Here it is!" announced Marcus, as they emerged from the main entrance of the commandant's house. "The fort!"

Gaius stood and stared open-mouthed. It had been dark when they'd arrived the night before, and besides, he'd been asleep in the wagon. He'd expected to see an army camp with lines of tents,

like the ones he'd seen before. This looked like a small town!

Marcus and Gaius were standing by the side of a broad road. Along both sides of the road were a mixture of stone and

wooden buildings. At the end of the road Gaius could see the high wall that surrounded the fort and a large gateway. A troop of soldiers were marching along the road towards the gate, led by a tall man on a horse. Each soldier had a javelin slung over one shoulder and a big curved shield strapped to his back. The tall man on the horse saluted to Marcus as they passed. Rumbling along the street in the opposite direction was a farm cart pulled by two massive oxen.

Marcus nodded towards the cart. "Supplies for the granary - over there -"

He pointed to a large stone building
further up the street. It had a wide, sloping
roof, and wooden shutters covered all the
windows.

"That's where all the grain is stored,"
explained Marcus. "There are more than
a thousand men on this fort, and that
means a *lot* of bread."

"A *thousand...*?" Gaius tried to
imagine a thousand men. He hadn't
realised that there were that many people
in the whole world.

"And that's where they eat and sleep."
Marcus pointed to a long line of low, one
storey-buildings standing end-on to the
broad street. "A hundred men in each
barracks," he continued, "plus their
centurion."

"And down here,"
he went on, "is our
Headquarters."

Marcus strode
off. Gaius tried to
follow him, but the
big dog had got
bored and sat
down. Gaius
tugged at the
lead.

"Oh, Finn...," groaned Gaius,
"—*please*?"

The dog just looked at him, yawned
and lay down.

"Here, boy!" bellowed Marcus.
"Here, Finn!"

The dog's ears pricked up, and with
a joyful bark he bounded after his master,
dragging Gaius behind him.

Marcus was standing in front of a
low wall. Through the small gateway,
Gaius could see a broad courtyard in front
of a squat, two-storey building.

"This is the HQ," explained Marcus, "the Headquarters, where the Camp is run from, the centre of everything. And over there is —"

He stopped. A short, muscular man in a red tunic was hurrying towards them. His face was as red as his tunic. He looked very cross about something.

"Severus," said Marcus, "this is my son, Gaius. Severus is our Quartermaster. He keeps us all fed, and equipped.

Anything we need, Severus gets us - right Severus?"

"When I'm not being robbed blind by the natives!" snorted Severus. "Did you see that wagon load of wheat that just came in?"

Marcus nodded.

"Well, it isn't what *I'd* call wheat," continued Severus. "Most of it is blown or rotten with mildew."

"Typical Brits," snapped Marcus, getting annoyed too. "You'd think they'd be grateful to us after all we've done for them - but are they? Huh! Right, Severus, I'll come with you and see to this thieving Celt - just in case the rest of them think that a new Prefect is a chance to get up to their old tricks!"

He turned to Gaius. "This shouldn't

take long. You wait here with Finn." He
turned on his heel and began to stride off
towards the granary. He stopped, and
shouted back to Gaius, "And don't go
wandering off!"

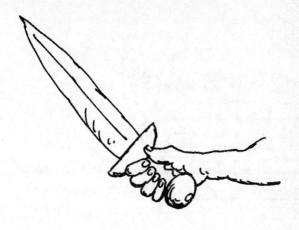

## 2

## Finn Escapes

Gaius looked down the road once again. There was no sign of his father. It felt like he'd been waiting for hours, and the wind was getting colder. He hugged his new leather cape tightly round him. He watched as a large cart loaded with straw

rumbled slowly past him. He waited, and
waited, and waited. Eventually the cart
rumbled back, empty. A couple of Britons
staggered past, their arms full of long
wooden poles. Gaius watched them until
they disappeared round the corner at the
far end of the street.

"Come on," Gaius muttered, "come
on!

He stamped his feet on the ground.

His leather leggings stopped just below the knees, and his calves were covered with goose pimples. He looked down at Finn. The dog was slumped in a bored heap, with his ears sagging.

"Come on, Finn," he jerked the lead. "Let's walk down to the granary."

The big dog clambered slowly to its feet and, for once, plodded along obediently at Gaius's side.

Gaius was just about to cross the narrow alleyway

separating the Headquarters and the granary when he heard *Thwack! Thwack! Thwack!*

Then a loud voice bellowing, "Come on, you useless cartload of wet lettuces! Put your backs into it! You can't tickle around like a load of serving wenches when you've got five hundred screaming blue Picts charging at you! Here - I'll show you - like this —" and there was a much louder *Thwack!* followed by the sound of splintering wood.

Cautiously, Gaius crept down the alleyway and looked round the far corner.

Behind the granary and the Headquarters building was a large open space. Four logs, about the height of a man, had been driven into the ground. The logs had big chunks hacked out of

 them. Standing around the scarred logs was a small group of legionaries carrying swords and shields. Despite the cold wind, Gaius could see that the young soldiers were sweating. Some were panting for breath and their shields were drooping. Standing to one side was an enormous bearded man with a deep scar across his forehead.

"Come on, *again!*" he yelled. "And this time put some force into it! *And keep those shields up*! How many times do I have to tell you? It'll be too late to practise when

you've got four foot of barbarian spear
through your guts! Right! Once more—"

But before they could begin, Finn
suddenly leapt forward, dragging the lead
out of Gaius's hand. Gaius watched
helplessly as the big dog galloped across
the exercise ground and disappeared into
the cluster of barrack blocks on the far
side of the square.

"Finn!" screamed Gaius, running after the dog. "*Stop!*"

"Oi, you!" yelled the soldier in charge, as Gaius ran past, "Stop!"

He ran after Gaius and grabbed the hood at the back of Gaius's leather cape.

"What are you up to?" demanded the old soldier.

"The dog —" gasped Gaius. "It's the prefect's dog - and I've got to catch him."

"Oh, yes," said the old soldier suspiciously. "And how come you happen to be chasing after the prefect's dog?"

"I'm - I'm- his son!"

The old soldier immediately dropped the hood. "I'm sorry, youngster, but you can't be too careful. Brits running round all over the fort,

stealing anything that isn't nailed down."
The big man looked very embarrassed.

"I've got to find him," shouted Gaius
as he ran on, "or my father will be furious!"

"Too right," murmured the old
soldier under his breath. "Too right!"

Gaius sprinted off across the square
towards the maze of buildings on the far
side of the camp.

## 3

## A Soldier's Joke

Gaius wandered round the identical
barrack blocks calling Finn. There was no
sign of the big shaggy hound.

"What *am* I going to do?" thought
Gaius.

He wandered back to the big road.

He looked round. There were the
barracks, lined up facing the gateway.
But there was no granary, and no
Headquarters building. He was lost. Gaius
felt the sharp sting of tears. He rubbed his
eyes fiercely and tried to pull himself
together. This wasn't how a legionary
would behave. Legionaries were brave and

tough. Gaius took a deep breath and tried to remember all the things his father used to say to him when he'd fallen over as a tiny child and grazed his elbow or his knee. "If you want to be a soldier, you have to put up with being wounded..." – "Soldiers don't cry. Soldiers don't panic."

Gaius took another deep breath and

counted to ten. Should he try and find his way back to the Headquarters and his father, or should he try and find the missing dog? Then he remembered something else his father had said to him, "A soldier looks after his arms and his animals first."

Gaius pulled back his shoulders. "By the left," he said to himself, "quick march!"

He marched over to a big gateway in the wall where a bored-looking soldier was standing guard.

"Excuse me," said Gaius politely.

"Yes," said the soldier.

"What do you want?"

"Have you seen a big, shaggy dog run past here."

"I might have done," said the soldier gruffly. "What's it to you sonny?"

"It belongs to the new camp prefect," replied Gaius. "I was - err- looking after it, and it - erm - sort of, ran off."

"Hmph!" grunted the soldier. "Doesn't sound to me like you were looking after it very well." The soldier looked very stern. Gaius looked down at his feet, ashamed. That was just the sort of thing his father would say when he found out.

Another soldier appeared from the far side of the gateway.

"What's the matter?" he asked.

"This lad's lost the prefect's dog," said the first soldier.

The second soldier smiled. He seemed much friendlier than the first soldier.

"Well, lad," he said, "there *is* a place in the camp where all the old dogs, especially the strays and runaways, end up eventually." He paused and grinned.

"Where?" asked Gaius excitedly. Maybe things would turn out alright after all.

"If you follow the wall all the way round you'll come to a small stone building on the far side of the fort. It's built into the wall. You can't miss it. There are no other buildings in the fort that look like it, and no other building on the fort that smells like it!"

And both soldiers laughed heartily.

"And that's where all the runaway dogs are kept?" asked Gaius.

"That's right," said the friendly

soldier. "Hope you find the dog you're looking for!" Both soldiers laughed again.

"Thanks very much," said Gaius, hurrying off along the roadway beside the wall.

Behind him he could hear the soldiers still chuckling.

Gaius stopped outside the small oblong building. It seemed too large and too well-built to be a kennel. "There can't be *that* many runaway dogs on the fort, can there?" he thought to himself. He looked at the small building suspiciously. But the soldier on the gate had been very sure, and Gaius had followed his directions carefully. And the soldier was right, it did smell a little, well, *peculiar*. It had to be the right place. Gaius shrugged, and walked through the low doorway.

He found himself in a small room with white-washed walls. Along each side wall ran what appeared to be wooden benches with large holes cut into the seat with spaces between. Down the centre of the floor were two channels of running water.

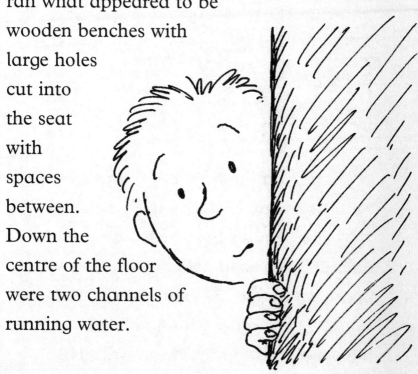

Sitting on the bench to Gaius's right were two soldiers chatting. Their short leather leggings were bagged around their ankles. They each held a short stick which had a sponge on the end. To Gaius's left was the old soldier who had been teaching the young legionaries sword drill. His

breeches were round his ankles too.
His sponge stick was standing in a small
hole in the stone floor in front of him. He
was leaning slightly forward with a look of
tremendous concentration on his face.

Gaius stood there open-mouthed.

The old soldier finally noticed him.

"It's you again, youngster," he said. "What's the matter? Haven't you ever seen a latrine before?" He chuckled heartily.

"B-b-b-ut," stammered Gaius. He blushed with embarrassment.

"What's the matter, lad?" asked one of the other men.

"The soldier at the gate said that this is where I'd find runaway dogs!"

All three men laughed.

"Oh he did, did he?" said the old soldier. "Dogs, did he say?

I'll be having a few words with him!"

He laughed again.

Gaius still looked confused.

"A soldier's joke, youngster,"
explained  the big man. "Like sending a
new recruit down to the Quartermaster to
ask for elbow grease." He chuckled again.
"But you can stop worrying about the dog.
I saw your father a few minutes ago.

The dog turned up. Now your father is looking for *you*, and he didn't look very pleased!"

Gaius's face fell.

"Don't look so worried, lad," said the old soldier kindly. "I've finished here. Give me a minute and we'll go and find your father together.

He stood up.

Gaius looked down at his feet, embarrassed, as the big man cleaned himself vigorously with his sponge. Then he rinsed it in the channel of running water.

"Right, youngster," he said, tying up his breeches again. "Time to find your father - and face the music!"

**4**

## An Old Soldier's Opinion

The big soldier led the way back from the latrine to the main road. They walked slowly past the commandant's house to the Headquarters building. Marcus was standing outside on the pavement looking up and down the street.

"At last!" he exclaimed when he saw
Gaius. "Where have you been skulking?
Finn came back hours ago!"

"I-I-I-" began Gaius. But Marcus was
far too cross to wait for an explanation.

"How dare you let a valuable dog like
Finn run off!" he thundered. "And then to
run away and hide like a deserter! I'm
ashamed of you!"

*A deserter!* Gaius felt hot tears of
shame spring to his eyes.

"If you'll let me say something, sir...?"
began the old soldier.

"Yes, Drusus," snapped Marcus. "What is it?"

"Well, I've run into the lad many times today," said the big man, "and I can vouch for him that he's been searching throughout the camp for that dog. He's stuck to his duty like a good 'un, if you don't mind my saying so."

"Hmmph!" grunted Marcus.

"And he's put up with a fair bit of teasing from some of the soldiers. I'd say that he's coped better with his first day on the fort than most of our new recruits. In fact, I'd rather have a plucky lad like him under my command than some of the milk-sop, mummy's-boys we get in the legions nowadays!"

"Well...." Marcus still looked annoyed, but the old soldier's opinion

seemed to have soothed him a bit.

Marcus looked down at Gaius. "If the First Spear thinks you've done alright, then I suppose you must have done." He paused and looked up at the sullen grey sky. He sighed. "It's too late to go hunting now. Drusus and Severus are coming to eat with us this evening. Perhaps it would be a good idea to go to the bath house and relax a bit before dinner. Will you join us, Drusus?"

"Be glad to," replied the old soldier, with a grin.

As the three of them set off down the main street Gaius yawned.

"It's been a busy day for a new recruit, eh lad?" The big senior centurion winked at Gaius. "I expect you're dog-tired, aren't you?" And he laughed loudly at his own awful joke.

# Roman Army Life

The Roman army was the biggest and best of its time. Soldiers were very well trained and well equipped. The Roman army was made up of the legions and the auxiliary troops. Only Roman citizens were allowed to join as legionaries, others could join up as auxiliaries. The auxiliaries were

organized into units of 500 or 1000 men. They were paid less than legionaries and were not as well trained

## Roman Legions

A legion had about 5,500 men under the command of a legate. A legion was divided into smaller units, made up of 80 to 100 men, called centuries. They were commanded by a centurion. Each legion would have a silver eagle as its standard - the symbol of the Roman Empire. The eagle was carried into battle by a soldier called an *aquilifier*. If the enemy captured the eagle the legion was disbanded.

## Army Discipline

Army discipline was very strict. A soldier who ran away in battle would be beaten to death. If a soldier put his unit in danger he was punished by being stoned to death. If a legion disobeyed orders they were given less food to eat as a punishment.

Training was hard. Each day the whole legion would practise swimming, running, jumping, javelin-throwing and fencing.

Life was hard for a soldier. But some enjoyed the life and stayed in the army until they were too old to serve.

## The Fort

This story is set in a fort on Hadrian's wall in the North of England. It is called Housesteads, and in Roman times was called *Vercovicium*. You can visit the ruins of Housesteads and some of the other forts on Hadrian's Wall.

The fort and the rest of the wall were built by the soldiers in the legion. But after it was all finished the legions went back to their bases, leaving the auxiliaries to guard the wall. At the time of this story the Wall was nearly finished.

# Hadrian's wall

Hadrian's wall was named after the emperor
Hadrian who wanted proper frontiers at the borders
of the Roman Empire. It took about 10 years to
finish and stretched across the north of England. It
was built to keep out the northern tribes who often
made raids into the areas under Roman control.

The Wall was over 4.5 metres tall and 3
metres wide and had deep ditches with steep banks
along both sides. There were a number of forts, like
Housesteads, where the soldiers guarding the Wall
lived.